MW01048948

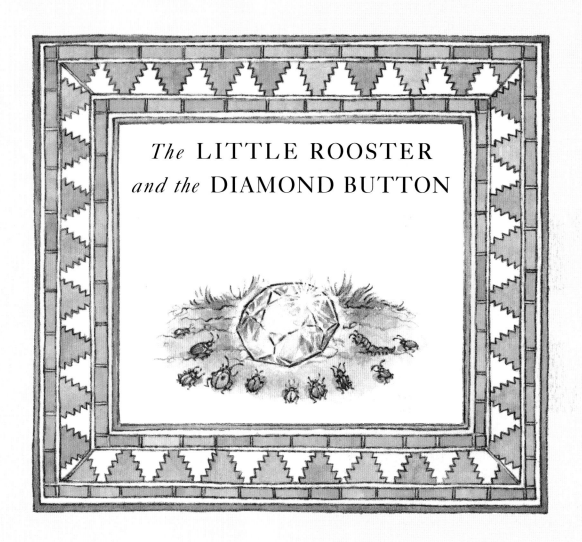

# The *LITTLE* ROOSTER
## *and the* DIAMOND BUTTON

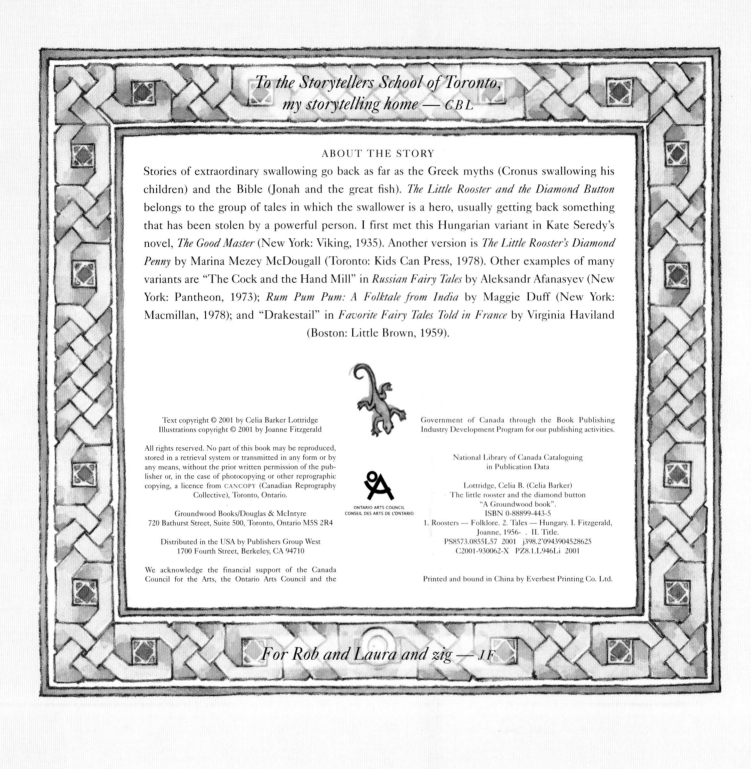

*To the Storytellers School of Toronto,*
*my storytelling home —* CBL

## ABOUT THE STORY

Stories of extraordinary swallowing go back as far as the Greek myths (Cronus swallowing his children) and the Bible (Jonah and the great fish). *The Little Rooster and the Diamond Button* belongs to the group of tales in which the swallower is a hero, usually getting back something that has been stolen by a powerful person. I first met this Hungarian variant in Kate Seredy's novel, *The Good Master* (New York: Viking, 1935). Another version is *The Little Rooster's Diamond Penny* by Marina Mezey McDougall (Toronto: Kids Can Press, 1978). Other examples of many variants are "The Cock and the Hand Mill" in *Russian Fairy Tales* by Aleksandr Afanasyev (New York: Pantheon, 1973); *Rum Pum Pum: A Folktale from India* by Maggie Duff (New York: Macmillan, 1978); and "Drakestail" in *Favorite Fairy Tales Told in France* by Virginia Haviland (Boston: Little Brown, 1959).

Text copyright © 2001 by Celia Barker Lottridge
Illustrations copyright © 2001 by Joanne Fitzgerald

All rights reserved. No part of this book may be reproduced, stored in a retrieval system or transmitted in any form or by any means, without the prior written permission of the publisher or, in the case of photocopying or other reprographic copying, a licence from CANCOPY (Canadian Reprography Collective), Toronto, Ontario.

Groundwood Books/Douglas & McIntyre
720 Bathurst Street, Suite 500, Toronto, Ontario M5S 2R4

Distributed in the USA by Publishers Group West
1700 Fourth Street, Berkeley, CA 94710

We acknowledge the financial support of the Canada Council for the Arts, the Ontario Arts Council and the Government of Canada through the Book Publishing Industry Development Program for our publishing activities.

ONTARIO ARTS COUNCIL
CONSEIL DES ARTS DE L'ONTARIO

National Library of Canada Cataloguing
in Publication Data

Lottridge, Celia B. (Celia Barker)
The little rooster and the diamond button
"A Groundwood book".
ISBN 0-88899-443-5
1. Roosters — Folklore. 2. Tales — Hungary. I. Fitzgerald, Joanne, 1956- . II. Title.
PS8573.O855L57 2001    j398.2'0943904528625
C2001-930062-X   PZ8.1.L946Li 2001

Printed and bound in China by Everbest Printing Co. Ltd.

*For Rob and Laura and zig —* JF

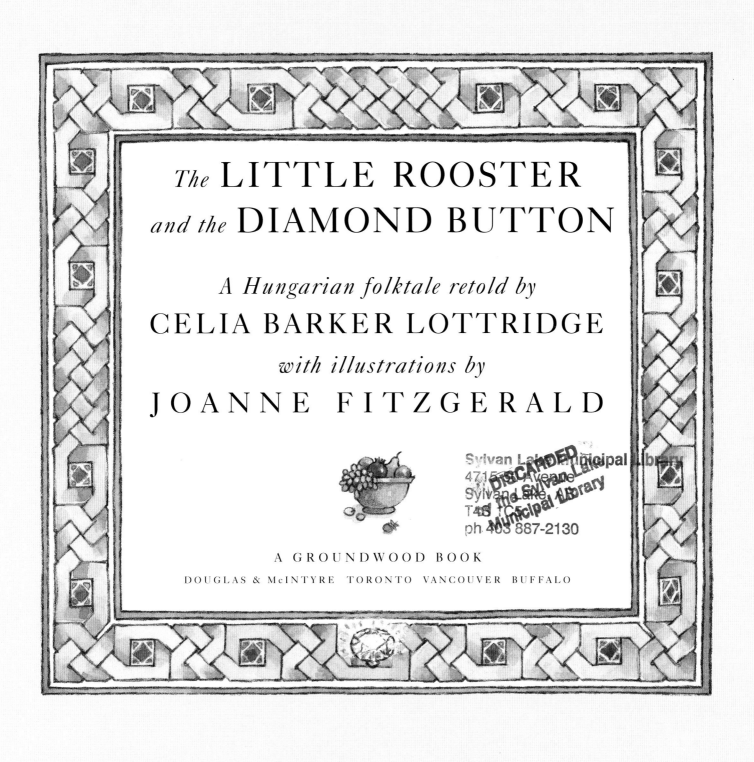

# The LITTLE ROOSTER
## and the DIAMOND BUTTON

A *Hungarian folktale retold by*

## CELIA BARKER LOTTRIDGE

*with illustrations by*

## JOANNE FITZGERALD

Sylvan Lake Municipal Library
4715 — 50 Avenue
Sylvan Lake
T4S 1C9 Central AB
ph. 403 887-2130

DISCARDED
by the Sylvan Lake
Municipal Library

A GROUNDWOOD BOOK

DOUGLAS & McINTYRE   TORONTO  VANCOUVER  BUFFALO

ONCE LONG AGO, a little rooster
lived with a poor old woman. The old
woman was so poor, in fact, that
sometimes she had nothing to feed the little
rooster. On those days he had to go out and
scratch for worms and bugs to eat.

Now the little rooster did not like to scratch in his own yard because the worms and bugs who lived there were his friends. So he would go out on the road to scratch for his supper.

One day while he was scratching, he saw something shiny lying there in the dust. The little rooster looked at it with one eye and then with the other eye. It was a diamond button!

"Cock-a-doodle-doo," said the little rooster. "I'll take this home to my poor old mistress. She would like to have a diamond button."

Just as he was about to peck up the button, down the road came the imperial sultan. He was the ruler of that country and he was very, very rich. He was dressed in silk from head to foot, he had rubies and emeralds on his fingers and gold chains around his neck. In his palace he had a room filled with heaps of diamond buttons.

But the sultan was greedy. When he saw the diamond button in front of the little rooster, he wanted that one, too.

He spoke to the three servants who were carrying a large silk umbrella to shelter him from the sun.

"Take that diamond button," he ordered. "I want it."

So the three servants put down the silk umbrella and rushed over and snatched the diamond button right out from under the little rooster's beak. They gave it to the greedy sultan and away they all went.

The little rooster was very angry.

"Cock-a-doodle-doo," he cried out. "Sultan! Sultan! Give me back my diamond button!"

But the sultan paid no attention. He disappeared down the road with his three servants holding the silk umbrella over his head.

The little rooster flapped his wings and followed. He flew and then he walked. He flew and then he walked until at last he came to the sultan's palace. He wasted no time but flapped his wings hard and flew up to a high window.

He stood on the windowsill and looked in. He could see the sultan sitting on a great carved chair. He was sipping cool mint tea from a golden cup and eating sweets from a silver bowl.

The little rooster flapped his wings, stretched his neck and crowed, "Cock-a-doodle-doo! Sultan! Sultan! Give me back my diamond button."

The sultan paid no attention.

"Cock-a-doodle-doo!" crowed the rooster, again. "Sultan! Sultan! Give me back my diamond button."

The sultan frowned. "Catch that little rooster," he said to his servants, "and throw him in the well."

So the three servants caught the little rooster and threw him into a deep, deep well.

But the little rooster had eaten nothing that day so he said, "Come, my empty stomach. Come, my empty stomach. Drink up all the water in the well." And his empty stomach drank up all the water in the well.

Then the little rooster flapped his wings hard and flew up to the window again.

"Cock-a-doodle-doo!" he said. "Sultan! Sultan! Give me back my diamond button."

The sultan was very annoyed.

"Catch that little rooster and throw him in the fire," he said in a loud voice.

The three servants caught the little rooster and threw him into the fire. But the little rooster said, "Come, my full stomach. Come, my full stomach. Let out all the water." And his full stomach let out all the water and the fire went out.

The little rooster flapped his wings and flew up to the window.

"Cock-a-doodle-doo!" he said. "Sultan! Sultan! Give me back my diamond button!"

The sultan was angry. He picked up two silk cushions and threw them against the wall.

"Catch that little rooster and put him in the beehive!" he shouted. "Let the bees sting him."

The three servants caught the little rooster and stuffed him in the beehive, but they left the door open, just a crack.

The little rooster looked at all the bees buzzing around

him and he said, "Come, my empty stomach. Come, my empty stomach. Eat up all the bees."

His empty stomach ate up all the bees. He could feel them buzzing around inside him. Then the little rooster flapped his wings and flew up to the window.

"Cock-a-doodle-doo!" he said. "Sultan! Sultan! Give me back my diamond button!"

The sultan was so furious he couldn't think. He stamped his feet and waved his arms.

"What shall I do with this little rooster?" he shouted. "WHAT SHALL I DO?"

"Lock him in the dungeon," said one servant.

"Sell him at the market," said another.

"I know," said the third. "You should SIT on him!"

"That's it," said the sultan. "I'll sit on him."

The three servants caught the little rooster and put him on the carved chair where the sultan liked to sit. And the greedy sultan SAT on him.

But the little rooster said, "Come, my full stomach. Come, my full stomach. Let out all the bees."

His full stomach let out all the bees. And did they sting the greedy sultan? THEY DID. The sultan jumped up.

"Ow!" he said. "Ow! Ow! Ow!" Then he shouted at the three servants. "Take this little rooster and give him what he wants. I never want to see him again!"

The three servants caught the little rooster and took him to the room that was filled with diamond buttons. They tossed him inside.

"Take what you want and go away," they said firmly. "We never want to see you again." And they left him there alone.

The little rooster looked at all the heaps and heaps of diamond buttons.

"Take what I want?" he said. "I think I will. Come, my empty stomach. Come, my empty stomach. Eat up all the diamond buttons."

The little rooster ate as many diamond buttons as he could hold. Then he started off down the road. He had to walk because he was so heavy with diamonds that he couldn't fly.

When he finally got home, the little rooster gave all the diamond buttons to the poor old woman, who was certainly very surprised. Then he went outside to tell his friends the worms and the bugs all about the sultan and his three servants and the diamond button.